This igloo book belongs to:

....

igloobooks

Published in 2020
by Igloo Books Ltd
Cottage Farm
Sywell
NN6 0BJ
www.igloobooks.com

0120 003
6 8 10 11 9 7
ISBN 978-1-78557-380-4

Illustrated by Nicola Anderson
Written by Jenny Woods

Cover designed by Kerri-Ann Hulme
Interiors designed by Jason Shortland
and Kerri-Ann Hulme
Edited by Stephanie Moss

Printed and manufactured in China

The Best Nest

Best
Nest
ontest

Judges

igloobooks

It was the day of the

Best Nest Contest.

Little Blue hopped with excitement, as birds from all around the world arrived to take part.

"I can't wait to get started," she chirped.

Eagle **soared** down and landed on a branch, knocking several little birds off it.

"I'm going to build a huge palace," he announced, grandly.

Kingfisher was busy admiring his reflection in the pond.
"My nest will be beautiful," he boasted, preening his
bright blue feathers. "Just like me!"

"You won't win!" squawked Parrot. "My nest is going to be amazing." Little Blue began to feel nervous. "I'll just try my best," she cheeped.

The other birds **twittered** with laughter.

As soon as the contest started, Eagle **zoomed** away.

He was in such a hurry, he didn't look where he was going.

Thwack!

He flew straight into a haystack.

Even though Little Blue was busy with her own nest, she fluttered over to help Eagle. "Never mind, Eagle," she said.

Then, Little Blue noticed all the bright yellow straw on the floor. She was just gathering it up for her nest, when a loud **squawking** sound made her jump!

It was Parrot and Kingfisher, fighting over a flower.
Little Blue went to see if she could help.

"I want it!"
screeched Kingfisher,
pulling hard.

"I found it!"
squawked Parrot,
tugging back.

Feathers flew as the two birds squabbled.

Thinking quickly, Little Blue scooped up some of the feathers.
"These are much prettier than petals," she said.
Kingfisher opened his beak to agree and let go of the flower.

With a **shriek** of delight, Parrot shot into the sky, clutching the flower in her beak.

"Huh!" huffed Kingfisher, **flapping** away. "I'll find something even prettier to decorate my nest with."

Little Blue had been so busy helping her friends, she hadn't even started building her own nest yet.

"My nest won't be anywhere near as good as the others," she worried. So, she got to work, but then, something caught her eye.

It was a paper cup...

... **hopping** along the ground.

Little Blue lifted it up and, to her surprise, underneath was Kingfisher. "Have you been rummaging through the rubbish?" asked Little Blue.

"I wanted pretty, shiny sweet wrappers for my nest," said Kingfisher, who was covered in sticky goo.

Little Blue held her beak while she helped
Kingfisher wash off the **smelly, gunky goo.**

Kingfisher was so pleased his feathers were fresh and sparkly
again, he offered Little Blue some sweet wrappers for her nest.

Grabbing the sparkly wrappers, Little Blue finally whizzed over to the nearest tree. "Oh dear," she said, looking at the odd bits and pieces.

"It's a funny mix of things to make a nest from, but I'll try my best."

Little Blue frantically set to work. "I'm running out of time!" she thought in a panic.

In the next tree,
Eagle had built a palace
so big, the branch
was starting to bend.

Kingfisher's nest was
smothered in shiny paper,
like a **giant** mirror.

The most amazing nest of all belonged to Parrot. It had seven wobbly floors, decorated in every shade of the rainbow. Parrot dropped her flower on the top.

The tower teetered and tottered, then...

... **CRASH!**

Little Blue rushed
over, but before she could
help Parrot...

... the whistle blew for the
end of the contest.

All the birds fell silent as the judge swooped down with the first prize trophy and handed it to...

... PEACOCK!

Eagle, Kingfisher and Parrot were outraged. They squawked rudely.

Then, there was a surprise announcement from the judge.
"The prize for Best Effort goes to... Little Blue!"
Little Blue was so amazed, she couldn't believe her ears.
She placed the trophy proudly in her nest.

A few weeks later, Little Blue was snuggled up in her nest when she heard a **tapping** sound. Her eggs were hatching and soon, the nest was full of fluffy little baby chicks.

"There isn't room for a trophy any more," thought Little Blue.

BEST EFFORT

Little Blue didn't need a trophy to know which nest was best.
"It's the one with my family in it," she said.